W9-AOV-018

DISCARDED

Property of
The Public Library of Nashville and Davidson County
225 Polk Ave., Nashville, TN 37203

DISCARDED

GOOD WORK, AMELIA BEDELIA

by Peggy Parish

pictures by Lynn Sweat

Greenwillow
Read-alone

Greenwillow Books
A Division of William Morrow & Company, Inc., New York

Text copyright © 1976 by Margaret Parish
Illustrations copyright © 1976 by Lynn Sweat
All rights reserved. No part of this book may be reproduced or utilized in any form or by any means, electronic or mechanical, including photocopying, recording or by any information storage and retrieval system, without permission in writing from the Publisher. Inquiries should be addressed to Greenwillow Books, William Morrow and Company, Inc., 1350 Avenue of the Americas, New York, NY 10019.

Printed in the United States of America.

19 20 21 22 23 24 25

Library of Congress Cataloging in Publication Data
Parish, Peggy. Good work, Amelia Bedelia. (Greenwillow read-alone)
Summary: Literal-minded Amelia Bedelia does household chores and gets dinner ready.
[1. Humorous stories] I. Sweat, Lynn. II. Title. PZ7.P219Goe [E] 75-20360
ISBN 0-688-80022-X ISBN 0-688-84022-1 lib. bdg.

For Sam and David Rogers
with love

"Amelia Bedelia," called Mr. Rogers.

"Is the coffee ready?"

"Coming right up," said Amelia Bedelia.

She poured a cup of coffee.

She took it into the dining room.

"There," said Amelia Bedelia.

"Would you like something more?"

"Yes," said Mr. Rogers.

"Toast and an egg."

"Fine," said Amelia Bedelia.

She went into the kitchen.

Very quickly

Amelia Bedelia was back.

Mr. Rogers picked up the egg.

He broke it over his toast.

"Confound it, Amelia Bedelia!"

he said. "I didn't say raw egg!"

"But you didn't say to cook it,"
said Amelia Bedelia.

Mr. Rogers threw down his napkin.

"Oh, go fly a kite," he said.

Amelia Bedelia looked surprised.

"All right," she said. "If you say so."

10

Soon Amelia Bedelia was out in a field.

She had a kite.

"Now that was nice of Mr. Rogers,"
she said. "I do love to fly kites.
But I better get back.
Mrs. Rogers might need me."

Sure enough, Mrs. Rogers was calling,
"Amelia Bedelia."

"Here I am," said Amelia Bedelia.

"There's a lot to do,"
said Mrs. Rogers.

"Do you know how to make bread?"

"I make good corn bread,"
said Amelia Bedelia.

"No, I want white bread,"
said Mrs. Rogers.

"You are a good cook.

Just do what the recipe says."

"All right," said Amelia Bedelia.

"Here's a list of the other things
   I want you to do,"
   said Mrs. Rogers.
"I'll be out until dinner time."
"Don't worry," said Amelia Bedelia.
"I'll get everything done."
   Mrs. Rogers left.

"I'll start with that bread,"
said Amelia Bedelia.
She read the recipe.
"Do tell," she said.
"I never knew
bread did magic things."

Amelia Bedelia got everything
she needed.
Quickly she mixed the dough.

Amelia Bedelia

set the pan on the table.

"Now," she said,

"you're supposed to rise.

This I've got to see."

Amelia Bedelia sat down to watch.

But nothing happened.

"Maybe you don't like to be watched.

I'll come back," said Amelia Bedelia.

"Let's see."

Amelia Bedelia got her list.

"Clean out the ashes

in the parlor fireplace.

Fill the wood box."

Amelia Bedelia went into the parlor.

She cleaned out the ashes.

And Amelia Bedelia filled

the wood box.

"That's done," said Amelia Bedelia.

"What's next?"

She read, "Pot the window box plants.

Put the pots in the parlor."

Amelia Bedelia went outside.

She counted the plants.

Then she went into the kitchen.

"My goodness," she said.

"I need every pot for this."

So she took them all.

Amelia Bedelia potted those plants.

And she took them inside.

"Now I better tend to that bread,"
said Amelia Bedelia.
She went into the kitchen.
But the bread still sat on the table.
"Now look here," she said.
"You are supposed to rise.
Then I'm supposed to punch you down.
How can I punch if you don't rise?"
Amelia Bedelia sat down to think.
"Maybe that pan is too heavy,"
she said.
"I better help it rise."

Amelia Bedelia got some string.

She worked for a bit.

And that bread began to rise.

"That should be high enough,"

said Amelia Bedelia.

"I'll just let you stay there awhile."

Amelia Bedelia picked up her list.

"'Make a sponge cake.'"

Amelia Bedelia read that again.

"I know about a lot of cakes,"
she said.

"And I never heard tell of that.
But if she wants a sponge cake,
I'll make her a sponge cake."

Amelia Bedelia put a little of this
and some of that into a bowl.
She mixed and mixed.
"Now for the sponge," she said.
Amelia Bedelia got a sponge.
She snipped it into small pieces.
"There," she said.
"Into the cake you go."

Soon the sponge cake was baking.

"I don't think Mr. Rogers

will like this cake,"

said Amelia Bedelia.

"I'll make my kind of cake too.

He does love butterscotch icing."

So Amelia Bedelia

baked another cake.

"There now," she said.

"I'll surprise him."

Amelia Bedelia put

the butterscotch cake in the cupboard.

She put the sponge cake on a shelf.

"My, this is a busy day,"
said Amelia Bedelia.
"Let's see what's next.
'Call Alcolu. Ask him to patch
the front door screen.'"
Amelia Bedelia shook her head.
"Alcolu can't patch anything,"
she said. "I better do that myself."
She got what she needed.

And Amelia Bedelia patched that screen.

Amelia Bedelia looked at the time.

"Oh," she said.

"I better get dinner started.

Let me see what she wants."

She read the list.

"'A chicken dinner will be fine.'"

Amelia Bedelia shook her head.

"What will she think of next?" she said.

"Well, that won't take long to fix."

Amelia Bedelia got everything ready.

She set the table.

Then she sat down to rest.

Soon Mr. and Mrs. Rogers came home.

"Amelia Bedelia," yelled Mr. Rogers.

"Coming," called Amelia Bedelia.

"What is that awful cloth
on the front door?" said Mrs. Rogers.

"You said to patch the screen,"
said Amelia Bedelia.

"Can't patch without a patch."

They went into the parlor.

"All my good pots!" said Mrs. Rogers.

"And bad ones too,"
said Amelia Bedelia.

Mr. Rogers looked at the wood box.

He shook his head.

But he didn't say a word.

They went into the kitchen.

"The sponge cake is pretty,"

said Mrs. Rogers.

"At least that's done right."

Something caught Mr. Rogers's eye.

He looked up.

"What in tarnation is that?" he said.

"The bread!" said Amelia Bedelia.

"I plumb forgot it.

Do let me punch it down quick."

She climbed up on a chair.

Amelia Bedelia began to punch.

Mr. and Mrs. Rogers just stared.

The bread plopped to the floor.

"Did I see what I thought I saw?"
said Mr. Rogers.

"You did," said Mrs. Rogers.

"Now," said Amelia Bedelia,

"dinner is ready when you are."

"Well, you can cook," said Mrs. Rogers.

"Dinner should be good."

"I hope so," said Mr. Rogers.

"I'm hungry."

"Just serve the plates,"

said Mrs. Rogers.

Mr. and Mrs. Rogers sat at the table.
Amelia Bedelia brought in the plates.

Mr. and Mrs. Rogers stared at the plates.

"But, but, that's cracked corn.

It's all kinds of awful things,"
said Mrs. Rogers.

"You said chicken dinner,"
said Amelia Bedelia.

"That's what chickens eat for dinner."

Mrs. Rogers was too angry to speak.

"Take this mess away,"
said Mr. Rogers.

Mrs. Rogers said,
"Serve the cake and coffee."
Amelia Bedelia did.

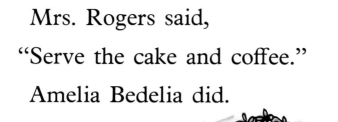

Mr. Rogers took a big bite of cake.

He spluttered and spit it out.

"What in tarnation is in that?" he said.

"Sponge," said Amelia Bedelia.

"Mrs. Rogers said

to make a sponge cake."

Suddenly Mr. Rogers laughed.

He roared.

Mrs. Rogers looked at the lumpy cake.

Then she laughed too.

"But I'm still hungry,"
said Mr. Rogers.

"I can fix that," said Amelia Bedelia.

"I have a surprise for you."

"Oh, no!" said Mr. Rogers.

"I can't stand another one,"
said Mrs. Rogers.

Amelia Bedelia brought in milk
and her butterscotch cake.

"Ahh," said Mr. Rogers.

"Hurry," said Mrs. Rogers.

"Give me some."

Soon the whole cake was gone.

"How do you do it, Amelia Bedelia?"
said Mr. Rogers. "One minute
we're hopping mad at you."
"And the next, we know we can't
do without you," said Mrs. Rogers.

Amelia Bedelia smiled.

"I guess I just understand your ways,"
she said.